Inspired by
Disney·PIXAR
TOY STORY 4

FORKY

in

CRAFT BUDDY DAY

Written by
Drew Daywalt

Illustrated by
George McClements and Stéphane Kardos

Disney PRESS

LOS ANGELES ● NEW YORK

Forky was Bonnie's favorite toy in the whole world. She had made him in kindergarten, and she took him everywhere she went.

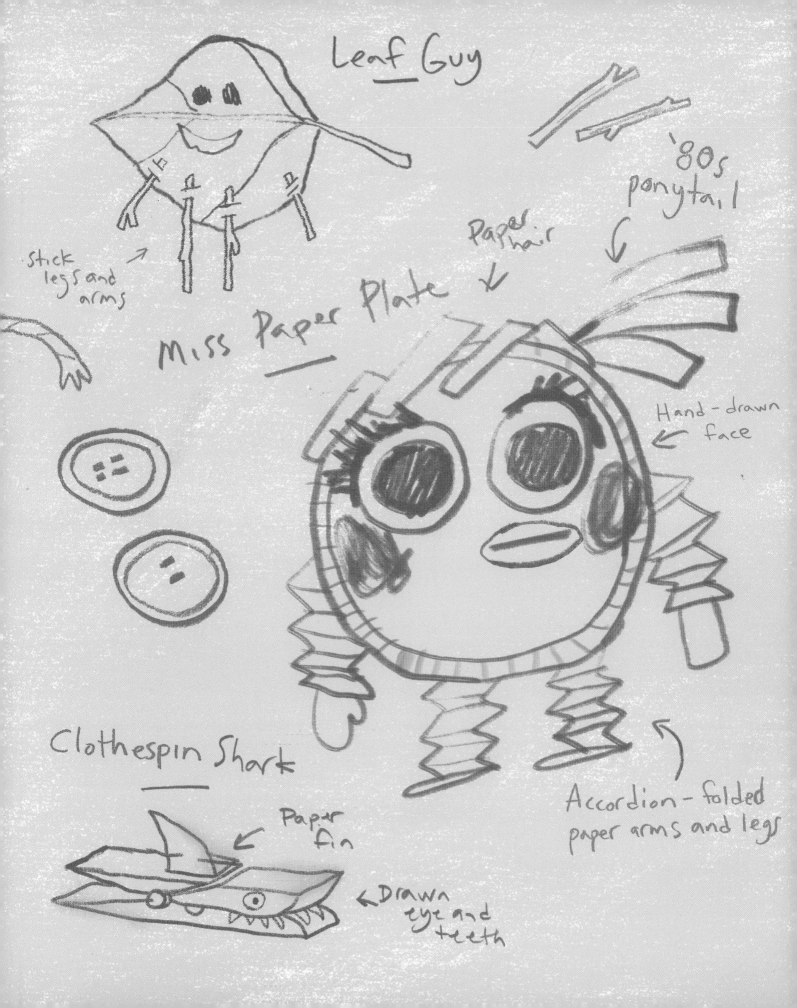

Leaf Guy

stick legs and arms →

Miss Paper Plate

Paper hair ↓

'80s ponytail ↓

Hand-drawn ← face

Accordion-folded paper arms and legs ↗

Clothespin Shark

Paper fin ←

← Drawn eye and teeth

At home, the other toys kept him company.

. . . and I was like, "Miranda, honey, you do *not* need him, girlfriend. That Garby Garbage Truck is just plain trash—" OOPS! I'm sorry, Forky! I know that's a sensitive subject for you.

Oh, that's okay! I know I'm a toy now.

Bonnie even took Forky to school with her.

But sometimes, like when Bonnie went to gym class or the library and Forky had to stay behind, he got lonely. And he kinda wished he had some friends to talk to when she was gone.

Then one day Miss Wendy made an announcement. . . .

I know everyone loves Forky. And Bonnie did such a fantastic job making him that I've decided today will be *Craft Your Own Buddy Day!*

Cool beans!

YAY!

Yeah!

Yippee!

Yay!

Hooray!

Miss Wendy took out all the art supplies and all the recyclables, and everyone got to work. Since Bonnie already had Forky, she helped everyone else with their projects.

Forky looked at all the things the kids were making.

It's too bad none of them can talk. Then they could *really* be my buddies. . . .

When the bell rang, Miss Wendy said, "Okay, everyone, time for recess! Don't forget to put your names on your craft buddies before you leave."

Yesss! Now they'll come to life, like I did when Bonnie wrote on me.

Forky watched the crafts lie there still and silent. Just as he was beginning to think they weren't going to come alive, all the craft buddies opened their eyes, sat up, and blinked in confusion. Then they started running around and screaming in panic!

As a Popsicle stick man flew past, Forky reached out and grabbed him.

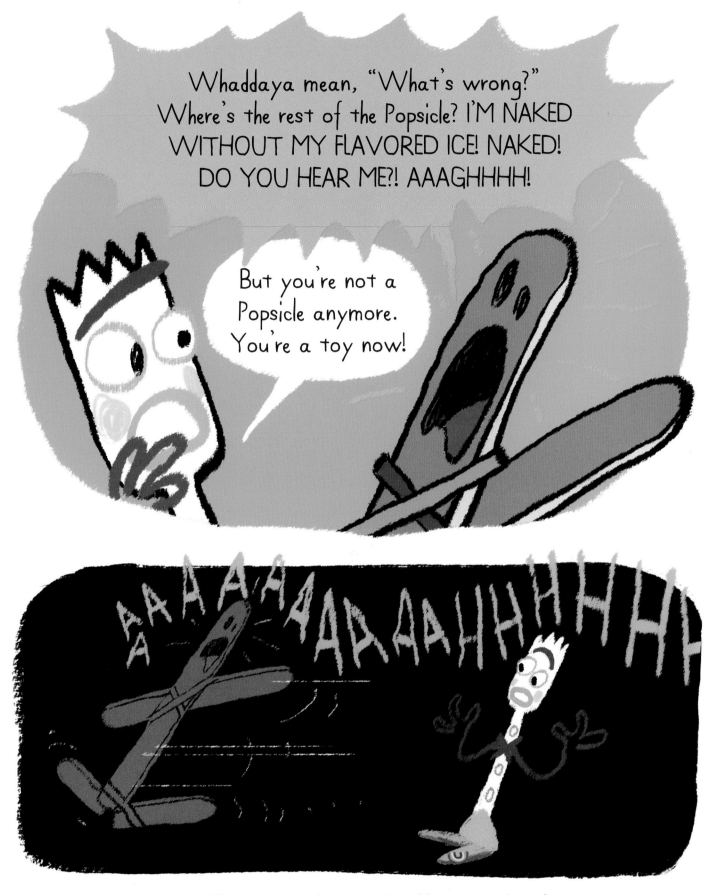

But Popsicle Stick Man just took off across the classroom, freaking out.

Next, Forky came face to face with a hand turkey.

Hi, I'm Forky.

I'm Mr. Chicken Fingers.

Chicken Fingers? But you're a hand turkey.

And you're a spork named Forky, but you don't see me complaining.

As Hand Turkey walked off, Miss Paper Plate ran up to Forky and grabbed him by the shoulders.

I NEED FOOD ON MY FACE, RIGHT NOW!

She reached into a nearby lunch bag, pulled out a bunch of cheese curls, put them on top of herself, and lay down flat.

Ahh, that's better. Now I look presentable.

Just as she said that, the paper bag jumped up, flipped upside down, and yelled at her.

HEY! Those are MY cheese curls!

But you guys aren't for holding food anymore.

As the bag and the plate wrestled over the cheese curls, a juice box robot rushed up and shoved its straw at Forky's mouth.

QUICK!

DRINK ME!

But you're empty! And you're not a juice box anymore!

Juice Box Robot didn't even hear him.

Forky looked down to see a clothespin shark at his feet, staring up at him.

Just then, Forky was almost run over by a toilet paper tube race car.

And with that, the race car zoomed off.

Forky looked around at all the craziness. Craft buddies were losing it everywhere. In the corner was Cloudy. . . .

Then there was Bubble Wrap Woman. . . .

And Leaf Guy . . .

B-R-R-I-N-G! The bell rang again. OH, NO! Recess was over and the kids would be back any second!

As Forky looked around, he knew that if the kids came back in and saw all the chaos, it would be a terrifying disaster! He had to calm down all the craft buddies and make them understand that they were toys, like, now!

But how?

chomp

chomp

chomp

All the craft buddies stopped and stared at him.

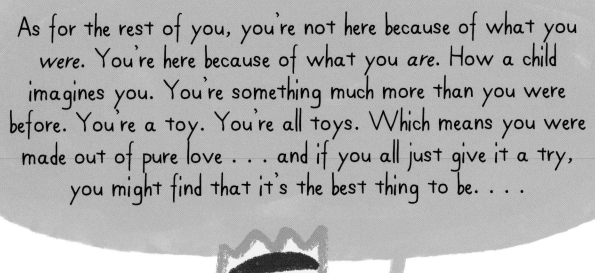

As for the rest of you, you're not here because of what you *were*. You're here because of what you *are*. How a child imagines you. You're something much more than you were before. You're a toy. You're all toys. Which means you were made out of pure love . . . and if you all just give it a try, you might find that it's the best thing to be. . . .

Suddenly, the classroom door was thrown open.
Miss Wendy, Bonnie, and the rest of the kids came in
to discover . . .

all the craft buddies lying there quietly in the same spots as before.

But as the kids took their seats at their tables, there was one thing that was different.

Each and every toy had
a smile on its face . . .

...especially Forky.

To Mom, for all the wonderful hours we spent crafting together —D. D.

For Rachel, Samuel, and Matthew —G. M.

To Tina, Magnus, and Nils —S. K.

Design by Winnie Ho

Printed in the United States of America

First Hardcover Edition, May 2019

10 9 8 7 6 5 4 3 2 1

ISBN 978-1-4847-9958-1

Library of Congress Control Number: 2018057266

FAC-034274-19088

For more Disney Press fun, visit www.disneybooks.com